KT-142-138

This edition published by Parragon Books Ltd in 2016

Parragon Books Ltd
Chartist House
15–17 Trim Street
Bath BA1 1HA, UK
www.parragon.com

© 2016 Spin Master PAW Productions Inc. All Rights Reserved. Paw Patrol and all related titles, logos and characters are trademarks of Spin Master Ltd. Nickelodeon and all related titles and logos are trademarks of Viacom International Inc.

ISBN 978-1-4748-3680-7

Printed in China

Action and Adventure

Three tales to enjoy...

Pups Save a Train
Pups Fight Fire
Pups Save the Party

Bath • New York • Cologne • Melbourne • Delhi
Hong Kong • Shenzhen • Singapore

Pups Save
a Train

Chase and Rubble are tidying up the Adventure Bay sandpit.

Rubble fills it with new sand, then makes a sand bulldozer for the children to play with.

"Wow, Rubble!"
says Chase.

"What can I say,
I'm a builder pup!"
says Rubble.

Meanwhile, Katie and her cat, Cali, are on the train home from Katie's grandma's house. Cali is reaching for a bag on the seat.

"Sorry, Cali," says Katie. "Grandma made these treats for the PAW Patrol."

Suddenly, the train starts shaking. There's a rockslide on the tracks! The train has to stop.

Katie calls Ryder for help.

"The PAW Patrol is on the way," says Ryder. "No job is too big, no pup is too small!"

Ryder calls the PAW Patrol to the Lookout. The pups rush to the control room and line up in their uniforms.

"PAW Patrol is ready for action, Ryder, sir!" says Chase.

Ryder tells the PAW Patrol that the train is trapped at the old bridge.

"We've got to get Katie home safe," he says.

Ryder needs Rubble and his digger to scoop up the rocks, and Rocky and his garbage truck to take the rocks away.

"I'm ready to dig it!" calls Rubble.

"Green means go!" barks Rocky.

Ryder, Rubble and Rocky zoom to the bridge at top speed.

Katie is waiting on the train. She's very happy to see her friends!

"Ryder and the PAW Patrol are here, Cali!" says Katie.

But Cali doesn't hear. She's watching a seagull outside eating a treat.

Then, Cali climbs right out of the train window and follows the seagull!

Ryder and the pups look all around, checking that the train tracks aren't broken.

"The tracks are okay," says Ryder. "We just need to clear the rocks so we can get the train off the bridge!"

Let's dig it!

"Rubble on the double!" barks Rubble.

He uses his digger to scoop the rocks into Rocky's truck.

Ryder hurries down the hill to take a look at the bridge.

"Rocky!" Ryder says through his helmet mike. "A beam has cracked. If it breaks, the train will fall!"

"We can prop up the bridge with a log," says Rocky. "But my truck won't be able to carry it down the hill – it's too steep!"

"We need an extra set of paws," says Ryder.

Ryder calls the other pups back in the Lookout.

"Chase!" says Ryder. "I need you and your truck at the bridge as soon as possible."

"Chase is on the case!" barks the pup, jumping into his police truck.

When Chase arrives, Ryder and Rocky
are tying a rope around an enormous log.

"Hi, Chase," says Ryder. "We need your
winch to lower this log down to the bridge.
We'll use the log to hold up the broken beam."

Chase attaches the log to the winch.
Then, Rubble uses his digger to push
the log over the edge of the hill.

At the bottom of the hill, Ryder and Rocky move the log into place.

"That's perfect," says Rocky. "It will hold until we get the train off the bridge."

Just then they get a call from Katie on the train.

"Cali is missing," says Katie.

"Don't worry, Katie," Ryder reassures her, "Chase will find her."

Cali is on top of the train, hoping to steal some bread from a seagull, when she slips!

"Meow!" Cali cries, hanging on with just one paw.

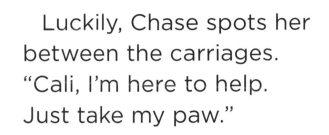

Luckily, Chase spots her between the carriages. "Cali, I'm here to help. Just take my paw."

Phew! The PAW Patrol has cleared the track and Cali is safe, too. The train can get moving again!

Later, Katie, Ryder and the PAW Patrol are in the park.

"Thanks, Ryder, thanks, PAW Patrol," says Katie, as she gives the pups their special treats.

"You're welcome," say the pups. "Whenever there's trouble, just yelp for help!"

The End

Pups Fight Fire

Marshall is training for the
Fastest Fire Pup trophy.

"Hose out!" barks Marshall
and he takes aim. He shoots
water straight into a bucket.

"Go, Marshall, go!"
cheer the other pups.

Next, Marshall gets his fire truck ready to rescue Cali from a tree.

But as he climbs up the ladder, it hits the tree and Marshall falls with a *BUMP!*

I'm okay!

Ryder is watching from the Lookout.

"It looks like Marshall could use a helping hand," he says, pushing a button on the PupPad. "PAW Patrol, to the Lookout!"

In the control room, the pups are ready for action.

"Marshall, you need our help today," says Ryder. "But we just want you to try your best and not worry about winning."

"Try my best and forget the rest!" says Marshall.

"Rocky, can you find something in your recycling pile to fix Marshall's ladder?" asks Ryder.

"I'm on it!" says Rocky.

The pups race out of the Lookout.

Rocky parks his truck next to Marshall's fire truck. He finds something he can reuse.

"Don't lose it – reuse it!" says Rocky.

"This broom will work," barks Rocky. "I'll use the handle to make new rungs for your fire ladder, Marshall."

Rocky screws the new rungs into place.

Ryder gets a call on the PupPad.

"There's a TV crew waiting to film Marshall as he breaks the Fastest Fire Pup record," says Mayor Goodway. "Marshall is late!"

The PAW Patrol has to get Marshall to the starting line right away.

Chase sounds the siren on his police truck and uses his traffic cones.

"My cones will stop the traffic until Marshall gets through," says Chase.

Marshall arrives just in time!

"Good morning, Adventure Bay!" says Mayor Goodway.

"Today, Marshall the Fire Pup will attempt to win the trophy for completing the Fire Rescue Course in the fastest time ever!"

"Hooray! Go, Marshall, go!" the crowd cheers.

"If Marshall can ring the City Hall's bell in less than 10 minutes," says the mayor, "he'll be the Fastest Fire Pup ever! Go!"

Marshall starts the race. "Do my best and forget the rest!" he says to himself.

First he completes the obstacle course. Then he uses his ladder. The new rungs mean that Marshall can easily reach the tree and rescue the toy cat.

Marshall races to
the next task on the
Beach Boardwalk.

"Hose out!" barks
Marshall. He takes
aim and the stream
of water puts out
a fake campfire.

"Go, Marshall!" the crowd cheers.

"I did it!" says Marshall. "Now I just have to get to City Hall and ring the bell."

But just as Marshall is about to get in his truck, he spots a real fire.

"Fire!" barks Marshall. "I'll take care of that. Hose on!" Marshall puts out the fire with his Pup Pack hose.

"Thank you so much, Marshall," says Mayor Goodway.

"You've only got 30 seconds left now, Marshall!" calls Ryder. "Go for it!

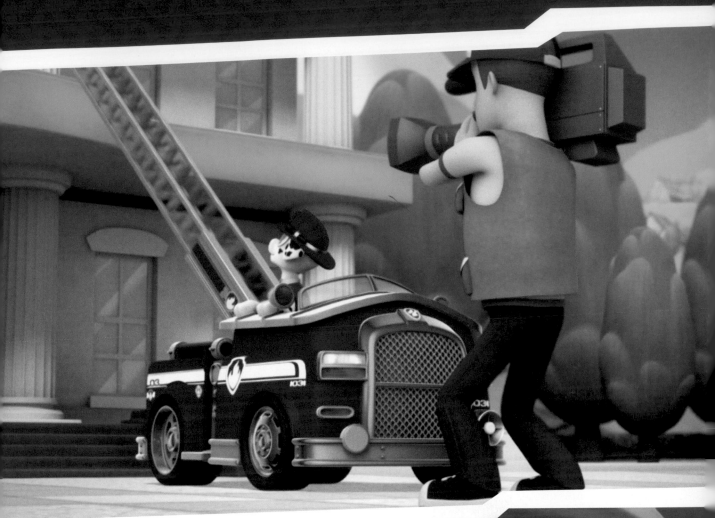

At City Hall, Marshall
races up his ladder to
the bell in the tower.

DONG!

But he's one minute
late! Poor Marshall hasn't
broken the record!
He feels disappointed.

"Marshall, you stopped to put out a real fire," says Mayor Goodway, "and that makes you an Adventure Bay hero!"

The mayor presents Marshall with the trophy. "For the Greatest Fire Pup in the World!" she says, and everyone cheers.

Later, back at the Lookout, the PAW Patrol is watching Marshall on the news.

"You did it, Marshall!" the pups shout.

Marshall is very proud of his trophy.
"I really did my *best*!" he says.

The End

Pups Save the Party

One windy afternoon, the pups are in Katie's Pet Parlour, busy preparing a surprise birthday party for Chase.

"Streamers away!" says Rocky.

"But who is keeping Chase busy and making sure he doesn't find out?" asks Skye.

"Marshall is," says Rubble. "He can keep a secret ... can't he?"

Marshall and Chase are at the park.

"It's too windy," calls Chase. "Maybe we should go and find the others."

"No! I mean, uh ... it's nice here," says Marshall. "It's not like there's a big secret I have to keep...."

Suddenly, the wind gets so strong, it blows the pups high into the air and on to the swings ... before they land back on the ground in a heap!

Thump!

Back at the pet parlour, everyone is still busy getting ready for the party. Suddenly, the lights go off!

"All the lights on the street are out, too," calls Rocky. "What happened?"

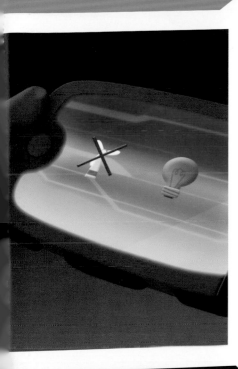

Ryder looks at his PupPad. "If the power is out, something must be wrong with one of the windmill turbines on Jake's Mountain."

"We won't have any music without electricity!" cries Skye.

"Or lights," says Rubble. "Maybe we can't have a party for Chase after all."

"No way!" says Ryder. He grabs his PupPad: "PAW Patrol to the Lookout!"

All the pups, including Marshall and Chase, race to the Tower. But there's no electricity, so the lift isn't working!

"Marshall," says Ryder. "I need to use your ladder to get up there."

Marshall raises his ladder and Ryder climbs up into the Lookout. He looks through the periscope.

"A windmill blade is broken," he says. "That's why there's no power."

"Pups, we have an emergency!" says Ryder. "Rocky, I need you to find something in your truck to fix that blade," he says.

"Marshall, we need your ladder to reach the windmill."

"Chase, the traffic lights will be out, too – we need your siren and megaphone to direct traffic."

"And Skye, Rubble and Zuma," he whispers, "you look after the party!"

The pups nod back.

"Let's do this!" bark the PAW Patrol.

Over on Main Street, the traffic lights aren't working.

There's a big traffic jam.

"We can't even cross the street," says Mayor Goodway, "it's already too dark."

Chase arrives and gets straight to work with his megaphone.

"WOOF!" he barks. "Everyone going this way, go now! All the cars going that way, stop!"

The drivers do as they're told and the traffic clears. The road is safe to cross.

Ryder, Marshall and Rocky are at the windmill.

"Let's get the electricity working for Chase's party," says Ryder, removing the broken blade.

"We can fix it with Zuma's old surfboard!" says Rocky. "Why lose it when you can reuse it!"

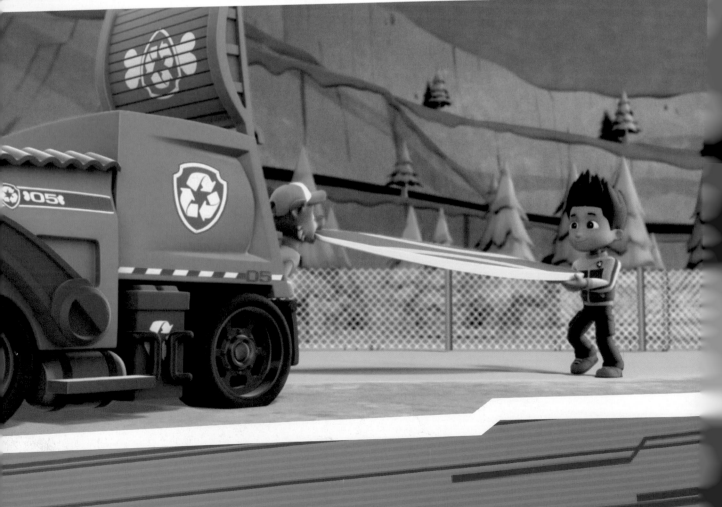

Marshall raises his ladder and Rocky climbs up. He attaches the surfboard to the windmill. Soon the wind picks up and it starts to turn.

"We did it!" shout Ryder, Marshall and Rocky together.

Back at the Pet Parlour, the pups are playing in the dark when the lights come back on. Everyone cheers.

"But it's too late to bake a birthday cake," says Skye.

"I have an idea," says Katie.

On Main Street, the traffic lights come back on.

"All right, everyone, it's safe to cross," says Chase.

"Thanks, Chase!" say the people on Main Street.

Just then, Ryder calls. "Chase. Change of plans. We need you at Katie's."

"On my way!" barks Chase.

Next, Ryder calls Skye. "Chase is on his way and so are we!" he tells her.

"Great!" says Skye. "The surprise is all ready."

When Chase arrives at Katie's Pet Parlour, all the lights are off.

"Hello, anybody home?" he calls.

"SURPRISE!" everyone shouts, jumping out from behind the counter. "Happy Birthday, Chase!"